W9-BLV-197

Adapted by Mary Man-Kong

Based on the screenplay by Billy Frolick and Cal Brunker & Bob Barlen

Based on the story by Billy Frolick

Illustrated by Emi Ordás

A GOLDEN BOOK • NEW YORK

© Spin Master Ltd. PAW PATROL THE MOVIE and all related titles, logos, characters; and SPIN MASTER logo are trademarks of Spin Master Ltd. Used under license. Nickelodeon and all related titles and logos are trademarks of Viacom International Inc. All Rights Reserved.
Published in the United States by Golden Books, an imprint of Random House Children's Books, a division of Penguin Random House LLC, 1745 Broadway, New York, NY 10019, and in Canada by Penguin Random House Canada Limited, Toronto. Golden Books, A Golden Book, A Big Golden Book, the G colophon, and the distinctive gold spine are registered trademarks of Penguin Random House LLC.

rhcbooks.com

ISBN 978-0-593-37461-0 (trade)

Printed in the United States of America

10 9 8 7 6 5 4 3 2 1

2021 Edition

Ring! The phone rang at the Lookout.

"PAW Patrol," Ryder answered. "What's your emergency?"

"Something terrible has happened!" exclaimed a small dog named Liberty. "Humdinger is now the mayor of Adventure City!"

Humdinger had been the mayor of Foggy Bottom and had almost destroyed the town, so Ryder knew that the people of Adventure City needed help.

"Come on, pups—pack your things," Ryder called to the PAW Patrol. "Adventure City is in trouble! No city is too big, no pup is too small!"

All the pups were excited—except Chase. He had lived in Adventure City when he was younger, and he had scary memories of being alone there.

"I'm afraid if I go back, everyone will see that I'm still that scared little puppy, and not the hero they think I am," Chase said to Ryder.

Ryder told Chase it would be different now, and that the people needed their help. "Now, can I get a yelp?" asked Ryder.

"Ow-woooo!" Chase yelped.

Meanwhile, Mayor Humdinger wanted to put the "adventure" in Adventure City. He had organized a huge fireworks extravaganza, but it kept raining. After discovering that the local university was working on a machine called the Cloud Catcher, Mayor Humdinger decided to learn more.

"We use it to study clouds," Kendra, the chief engineer, told Mayor Humdinger.

But the mayor had a better idea: he would use the Cloud Catcher to take the clouds away so there would only be sunny days!

Soon the PAW Patrol arrived at a giant tower in the center of Adventure City.
"Welcome to our new Adventure City headquarters," Ryder said to the pups.
"Whoa!" they all yelped.

There were new vehicles and new outfits, and there was even a self-service pup-treat dispenser! "Ohhhhhh!" Rubble said happily. The rest of the PAW Patrol laughed.

At city hall, Mayor Humdinger used the Cloud Catcher to vacuum all the clouds away. Now the Adventure City fireworks show could begin! A technician pushed a button, and a few fireworks flew into the air. But Mayor Humdinger wanted bigger fireworks. He impatiently slammed a hand on all the buttons at once!

KABOOM! BOOM! BOOM!

Fireworks and rockets exploded in all directions, causing huge fires everywhere!

From their new headquarters, the pups saw smoke rising into the sky.

"We've got to stop those fireworks before they burn down the city!" said Ryder.

The PAW Patrol was on a roll! They suited up and were ready for action . . .

. . . until they got stuck in bumper-to-bumper Adventure City traffic!
All of a sudden, a small dog jumped into Ryder's vehicle.
"I'm Liberty," the dog said to Ryder. "We spoke on the phone.
I can get you out of this parking jam, but it ain't gonna be pretty."
As fireworks exploded everywhere, Liberty showed the team
a shortcut to city hall.

The PAW Patrol went straight to work. Marshall quickly pressed a button on a control panel in his truck, and huge water cannons appeared. "That's what I'm talking about!" he exclaimed as he started extinguishing the fires.

Rocky scooped up fireworks and put them in his recycling truck. They exploded, bouncing his truck all around. "Ride 'em, cowboy!" he called.

"The PAW Patrol? What are *they* doing in Adventure City?" Mayor Humdinger asked as he ran for cover.

Chase spotted a group of people trapped on a balcony and launched himself into the air. "Parachute deploy!" he commanded, dropping toward the group. But after he landed, the wind blew him off the balcony. His parachute caught on a ledge, and he was stuck hanging over the flames!

"Help!" he cried.

Marshall quickly shot his water cannon and put out the fire.
Then Ryder and the other pups helped get Chase and the
people down to safety.

Chase couldn't believe he had forgotten to disengage his
Pup Pack. He felt he had let everyone down. Luckily, the PAW
Patrol was able to stop the fire and save the day.

But Mayor Humdinger was upset. The PAW Patrol had stolen his spotlight! So the next day, he came up with another plan to become the star of Adventure City. He built the kookiest, swoopiest, loop-de-loopiest subway train track and named it the Humdinger Hyperloop. Before testing the system to make sure it was safe, he flipped the switch on an incoming train to move it to the loop track.

The unsuspecting passengers raced around the first loop, but just as they rounded the top of the second loop—**SCREECH**—the subway cars got stuck. The passengers were hanging upside down!

"Help, PAW Patrol!" they called.

The PAW Patrol was on the way! Liberty hopped into her squeaky wagon to join her friends.

"Reporting for duty . . . like an honorary member," Liberty said.

After Rocky and Rubble locked the loop into place and Skye secured the train to the tracks, Chase ran along the roof of the building near the dangling train to try to get the passengers down. He quickly scooted along the ledge, and then he suddenly realized how high up he was. He looked down and froze. He wasn't sure he could do it.

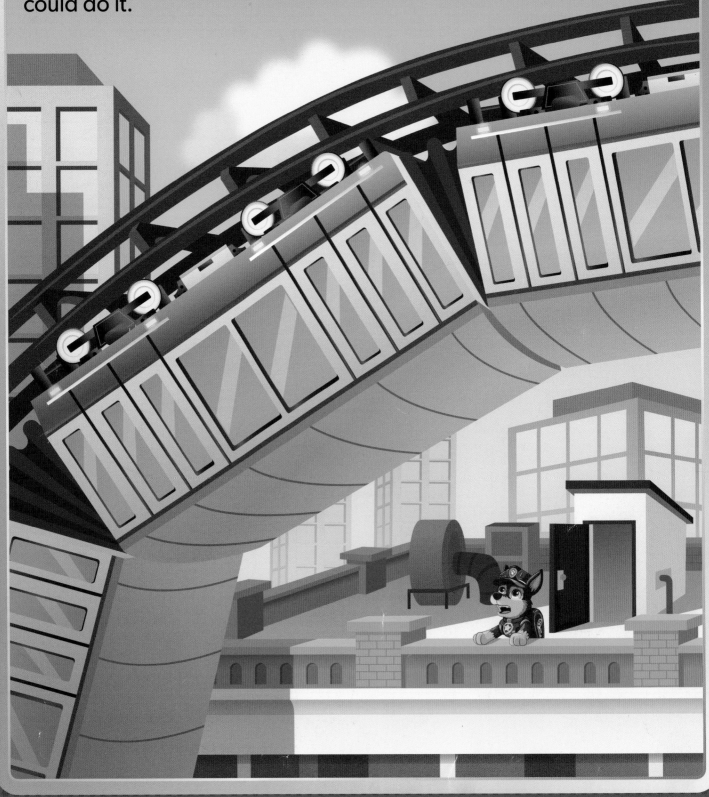

Skye saw that Chase was in trouble and radioed Ryder for help.
Ryder called Marshall to set up a sliding ladder to save the
passengers while Skye flew down to help Chase off the roof ledge.

Once everyone was safe, the crowd cheered. But Ryder was concerned about Chase.

"Maybe you need a break," Ryder said to his friend. "I have to know that I can count on you. Until you can get it together, I can't send you out on any more rescues."

Chase was hurt by Ryder's words. "You can't count on me? Well, I can't count on you!" Chase said, and he ran down the street.

Ryder ran after him, but when he turned the corner, all he found was Chase's tracking collar. Chase was gone!

BZZZZ! An electronic steel door locked behind Chase. Under Mayor Humdinger's new order to get rid of all dogs from Adventure City, Chase had been dognapped!

Chase looked around. He was locked in a dog jail with other dogs who had been dognapped!

Meanwhile, the PAW Patrol was desperately searching for Chase.

"Somebody must have seen something," Liberty said.

Then, at a small corner store, they learned that many dogs were missing.

"Humdinger!" Ryder exclaimed. "He hates dogs. But where is he taking them?"

Liberty had an idea. "I'm kind of an honorary member of the PAW Patrol," Liberty told them, "so I'll be the bait." She planned to get herself dognapped to lead the team to Chase.

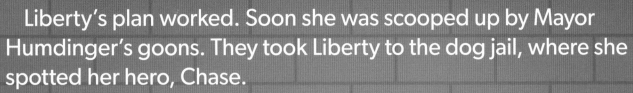

Liberty's plan worked. Soon she was scooped up by Mayor Humdinger's goons. They took Liberty to the dog jail, where she spotted her hero, Chase.

Chase didn't think he deserved to be rescued. "I used to think I was a hero," Chase told her. "It turns out I'm just scared."

"Heroes get scared," Liberty told Chase gently. "But they push through and keep going. That's what makes them heroes."

Chase felt better, but he told Liberty that the doors were locked and there was no way to escape.

"I forgot to tell you," said Liberty. "I brought backup."

BOOOOM!

Rubble's wrecking ball made a big hole in the wall. The dogs were free!

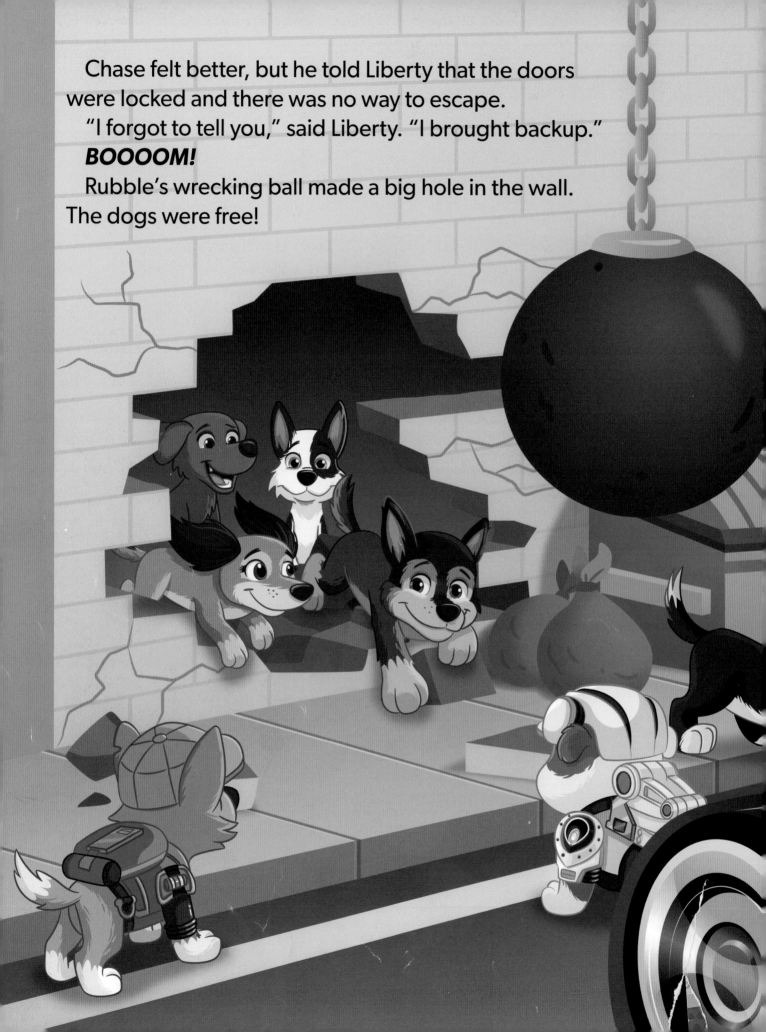

Ryder was happy to see Chase. Leaving the other dogs, Ryder took his friend to the corner where he had found Chase as a young pup.

"Why would you bring me here?" Chase asked, upset.

"You were too small to look after yourself, and you were scared, but I saw the bravest pup I'd ever seen," Ryder said, giving Chase a hug. "This is where I met my best friend."

Chase hugged Ryder back. "I won't let you down."

In front of a huge crowd, Mayor Humdinger revealed his next plan. He had created the tallest building in Adventure City by putting a new tower on top of the tallest skyscraper! He called it Humdinger Heights, and he made the top floor his office so he could keep an eye on the city.

Meanwhile, Kendra, the university engineer, tried to warn Mayor Humdinger about the Cloud Catcher. He had been using it nonstop, and it was operating at maximum capacity. It was going to explode!

But the mayor wouldn't listen. He stomped on the Cloud Catcher's remote control, destroying it.

Unfortunately, the rivets that held the Cloud Catcher together popped, and thick clouds started billowing out. **FLASH!** A giant lightning bolt lit up the sky. **FLASH! FLASH!** The overloaded Cloud Catcher unleashed weeks of bad weather in a single moment!

The PAW Patrol saw the storm from their headquarters and got ready to go to Humdinger Heights.
Liberty looked wistfully at her friends.
"Do you ever wonder what it would be like to be an official member of the team?" Ryder asked Liberty.

"Only, like, all the time!" Liberty said.

"But to do that, you'll need a faster vehicle," Ryder said, and he presented the little dog with a rocket-powered scooter.

Liberty couldn't believe it—she was going to be part of the PAW Patrol!

"Welcome to the team!" they cheered when Liberty roared up to them.

There was no time to waste! The wind had started to blow, and hail the size of basketballs fell from the sky.

"Liberty, Rocky, Marshall—get those people inside," said Ryder.

Suddenly, a school bus came flying toward them. "Deploy net!" Chase commanded as his net caught the bus.

"Good thinking, Chase!" said Ryder.

"You can count on me," said Chase.

Meanwhile, Ryder rushed to the top of Humdinger Heights and saved Mayor Humdinger, who had become trapped. But just as Ryder was leaving the tower, it tipped over and smashed onto a building across the street—with Ryder inside!

"I'm coming, Ryder!" Chase exclaimed as he jumped onto his motorcycle. His suction-cup tires engaged and he drove straight up the side of the building toward the gap.

Chase carefully climbed across the bridge. *"Don't look down, don't look down,"* he muttered to himself.

Then he pressed his Pup Tag to see if he could find his best friend.

"Ryder, this is Chase. Come in."

He saw a flashing light buried under a pile.

"Ryder, I see your light," called Chase. "Hang on!"

Chase used his grappling hook to get across the bridge, but a gust of wind blew the rope off course and toward the ground, dragging him over the bridge with it.

Dangling from the bridge, Chase tried to calm down. Thinking quickly, he said, "Disconnect Pup Pack!"

He was free—but he didn't have any more gear.

Knowing he had to help his best friend, Chase remembered what Ryder had told him. He said Chase was the bravest pup he'd ever seen.

Chase was scared, but he leaped across the huge gap and landed on the other side!

Chase ran up to Ryder, whose leg was stuck under a fallen slab of concrete. With some teamwork, they were able to get it free!

"I told you that you were a hero," Ryder told Chase. "Now come on. Let's get out of here."

Above Adventure City, Skye tried to get closer to the Cloud Catcher, but her copter blades became covered in ice. The Cloud Catcher was spinning wildly, and bolts of lightning were shooting everywhere!

Skye flipped some switches, and her copter transformed into a rocket, which sped closer and closer to the Cloud Catcher.

KABOOM! The Cloud Catcher exploded and blasted all the storm clouds away!

"But where's Skye?" Liberty asked.

The PAW Patrol looked up and saw something flying down. It was Skye—with her jet pack! She was safe.

Just then, the pups saw that Ryder was injured. They rushed over as he sat down, pouncing on him and licking his face.

"How do you feel?" Liberty asked, worried.

"Covered in drool," Ryder joked.

Everyone was going to be okay!

The next day, there was a big celebration at city hall.
Mayor Humdinger had been put in jail, and the PAW Patrol
was given a key to the city for all their hard work.
"Pup, pup, hooray!" they cheered.

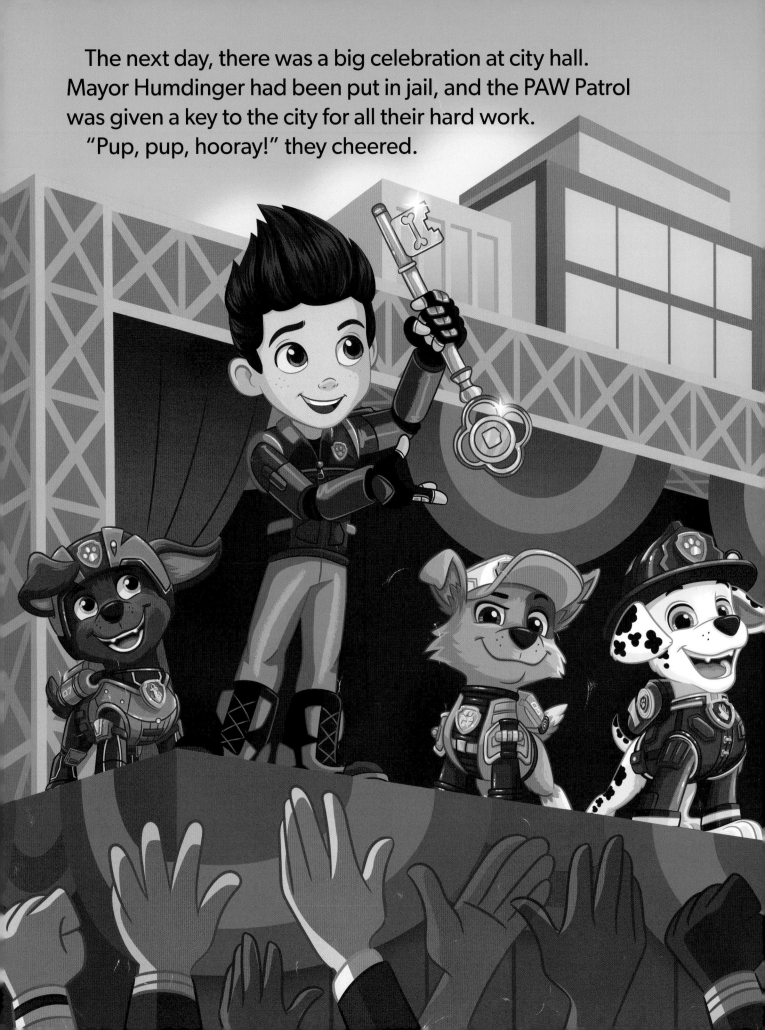

"Let's hear it for Marshall, Rubble, Chase, Rocky, Zuma, Skye—and the newest member of the PAW Patrol, Liberty!" said Ryder. Liberty looked out at the cheering crowd, happy that she had helped save her city!